Book

Hello, Crabby!

Jonathan Fenske

ACORN™
SCHOLASTIC INC.

For Pendy, who still laughs
at my dad jokes.

Copyright © 2019 by Jonathan Fenske

Library of Congress Cataloging-in-Publication Data

Names: Fenske, Jonathan, author.
Title: Hello, Crabby! / by Jonathan Fenske.
Description: First edition. | New York, NY : Acorn/Scholastic Inc., 2019. |
Series: Crabby | Summary: Crabby is not a happy crab, in fact Crabby is quite crabby,
so pushy Plankton, who is always trying to cheer up fellow marine creatures,
bakes Crabby a cake—but will Crabby finally smile?
Identifiers: LCCN 2018033264 | ISBN 9781338281507 (pbk) | ISBN 9781338281514 (hardcover)
Subjects: LCSH: Crabs—Juvenile fiction. | Plankton—Juvenile fiction. |
Cake—Juvenile fiction. | Cheerfulness—Juvenile fiction. | CYAC:
Crabs—Fiction. | Plankton—Fiction. | Cake—Fiction. |
Cheerfulness—Fiction. | Humorous stories. | LCGFT: Humorous fiction. |
Picture books. Classification: LCC PZ7.F34843 He 2019 | DDC (E)—dc23 LC record available
at https://lccn.loc.gov/2018033264

10 9 8 7 6 5 4 3 2 1   19 20 21 22 23

Printed in China   62

First edition, May 2019

Edited by Katie Carella
Book design by Marissa Asuncion

The **sun** in my eyes.

The **salt** in my teeth.

The **sand** in my shell.

2

3

Hmmm. What exciting thing can I do today?

I can dig a hole.

I can watch the ocean fill it up.

I can dig a hole **again**.

I can scuttle to the dunes.

I can scuttle to the water.

I can sit **right here**.

Wow.

So many choices.

Well, it looks like today is a **SCUTTLE-TO-THE-WATER** day.

THINGS TO DO:
scuttle to the water

5

Ugh.
There is that
boring Barnacle.

He is
always
hanging
around.

9

THE CRABBY CRAB

Oh, great.
Here comes that
pushy Plankton.

Good morning, Crabby!

Hmmmph.

I said, **good morning, Crabby!**

What is so **good** about it?

15

16

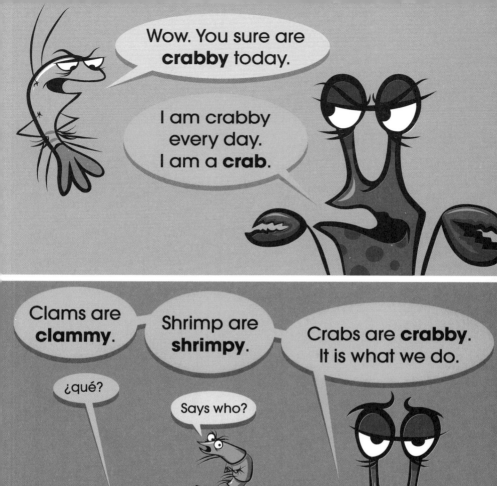

Well, Abby is a crab. And **she** is not crabby.

Tabby is a crab. And **she** is not crabby.

Blabby is a crab. And **he** is not crabby.

19

If I told you a **funny** joke, would you still be crabby?

Probably.

But it is a **really funny** joke.

Probably not.

21

So, you would probably **not** be crabby if I told you a really funny joke?

No. It is probably **not** a really funny joke.

I **promise** it will tickle your funny bone!

23

28

THE CAKE

Hello, Crabby!

If I told you I baked you an **awesome** cake, would you still be crabby?

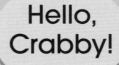

Why did you bake me a cake?

It is not my birthday.

I know.

It is not **your** birthday.

I know.

It is not
BAKE-YOUR-FRIEND-A-CAKE
day.

I know.

30

31

33

36

37

38

41

Well?

WELL?

WELL?!

It is a little **dry.**

AAARGH!

Crabby is **TOO CRABBY!**

About the Author

Jonathan Fenske lives in South Carolina with his family. He was born in Florida near the ocean, so he knows all about life at the beach! Sea creatures never baked him a cake, but he would have **loved** Plankton's cake because chocolate is his favorite flavor.

Jonathan is the author and illustrator of several children's books including **Barnacle Is Bored**, **Plankton Is Pushy** (a Junior Library Guild selection), and the LEGO® picture book **I'm Fun, Too!** His early reader **A Pig, a Fox, and a Box** was a Theodor Seuss Geisel Honor Book.

THESE BOOKS ARE NOT FUNNY.

Barnacle Is BORED
Jonathan Fenske

Plankton Is PUSHY
Jonathan Fenske

YOU CAN DRAW CRABBY!

YIPPEE.

1. Draw two ovals and connect them with a "U" to make eyes.

2. Draw the body.

3. Add six legs and one mouth.

4. Draw two arms and two claws. (One claw should be bigger.)

5. Add the details.

6. Color in your drawing!

WHAT'S YOUR STORY?

Plankton bakes Crabby a cake.
What kind of cake would **you** bake for Crabby?
What would your cake look like?
Would your cake make Crabby smile?
Write and draw your story!

scholastic.com/acorn